SHARED LOVERS EROTICA

THE MORE
THE Sexier

I0683879

JUST PLAIN BOB

WARNING

This book contains sexually explicit scenes and adult language. It may be considered offensive to some readers. This book is for sale to adults ONLY.

Please store your files wisely where they cannot be accessed by underage readers.

* * * * * * * * * * * * * * * * * *

WANT FREE COPIES OF MY BOOKS?
Just visit my blog and download free copies of my books:
awesomeauthors.org/justplainbob

About the Publisher

4Fun Publishing, a member of **BLVNP Incorporated**, 340 S. Lemon #6200, Walnut CA 91789, info@blvnp.com / legal@blvnp.com
NOTE: Due to the highly emotional reaction of some people to works of erotic fiction, any email sent to the above address that contains foul language or religious references is automatically deleted by our anti-spam software and will not be seen. All other communications are welcome.

DISCLAIMER

Please don't be stupid and kill yourself. This book is a work of FICTION. Do not try any new sexual practice that you find in this book. It is fiction and not to be confused with reality. Neither the author nor the publisher or its associates assume any responsibility for any loss, injury, death or legal consequences resulting from acting on the contents in this book. Every character in this book is over 18 years of age. The author's opinions are not to be construed as the opinions of the publisher. The material in this book is for entertainment purposes ONLY. Enjoy.

The More The Sexier

Shared Lovers Erotica

By: Just Plain Bob

© **Just Plain Bob 2015**
ISBN: 978-1-68030-440-4

Chapter 1

It was a surprise to me just as I suppose it was a surprise to every other man who finds out that his beloved isn't his alone. And, like most others who found out, I found out by accident.

I was in Chicago and had just closed the deal that was going to get me promoted to regional director. I called a good friend that I'd gone to school with and who lived in the Chicago area and whom I hadn't seen in quite a while. We had talked on the phone a lot, but hadn't had a face to face in ten years. I called him and asked if he be up to a drink or three and he said "Hell yes!"

I was at the Hilton and sitting at the hotel bar when he got there. I was working on a list when Barry walked up to me and I stood up to greet him and hug him and as I did the list fell to the floor. Barry bent and picked it up and saw that it was a list of girl's names.

"What's this, you old dog you? The list of honies you are going to call tonight to get them to come out and party with us?"

"Not hardly. When I go back to Denver I'll be moving into the regional director's office and I have to pick a personal assistant and these are the names of the finalists. I have to decide on one of them, but the problem is that they would all be good in the position. There isn't anything that would set one above the others."

Barry climbed on the bar stool next to me and asked. "How are they sexually?"

"What kind of question is that?"

"You ever have any deals where a bit of a sweetener would help?"

"I don't know what you are getting at."

"Three months ago we were working on a deal to purchase a whole lot of machine parts. There were three companies in the running for the contract and all had about the same thing going for them as far as price, quality and delivery schedules and the like. I was the junior member of the team and while my input was wanted, Cal and John were the guys who were going to make the decision. The guy from Martin asked what it was going to take to get the contract. Cal said:

"A night with your personal assistant."

"Cal was joking when he said it, but the guy from Martin said he would make it happen. Cal looked at John and John nodded a yes and Cal said make it happen and you have the contract."

"Did it happen?"

"Oh boy, did it ever. She was one hot babe for being in her forties. They were here for two days and she took us all on. One at a time, two at a time and even three at a time a couple of times. I can't wait for next year when it will be renewal time for the contract. I mean this babe was really hot. Even though I'm married I'd run off with her in a heartbeat."

"Martin, you say? I know a couple of people at Martin. Do you remember their names? Maybe I know her."

"His name was Dale and hers was Sandi. I remember that because whenever she was introduced to someone she would say "That's Sandi with an i.""

My pleasure in meeting up with Barry after so many years dimmed somewhat. My wife Sandi worked for Martin Industries and she was Dale Hartman's personal assistant.

Barry and I had several drinks together and then we had dinner and talked about old times, but my mind was on what he'd told me. Sandi made one or two trips a month with Dale. Had she been fucking people for contracts on all those visits? She had been with Martin almost twenty years and she had been Dale's assistant for the last ten of them. Jesus, what a bunch of questions that brought up. When did she start fucking around on me? Did she start after going to work for Dale or before? Did she limit her cheating for work or was she fair game for anyone? Had she fucked anyone that I knew? Any of my friends? Thank God we didn't have kids. At least the issue of who their father might be wouldn't have to be addressed. We had another drink after dinner and then parted company after promising to keep in closer touch.

I spent the night in my hotel room wondering if Sandi was sleeping alone while I was gone. On the flight home I thought about what I should do. Ignore it? Sandi and I had what I thought was a good marriage. She was very loving and affectionate toward me. Our love life was fine or at least I had thought it was. We averaged maybe three times a week and usually twice on a Saturday or Sunday and I didn't consider that to be all that bad considering we had been married for twenty-three years.

Should I ignore what I'd learned from Barry and operate on the principal that my life was good so don't do anything to change it? Even as I had the thought I knew I wouldn't go that way. Divorce? Did I really want to be single again at forty-five? I thought of all the women I knew in their early to mid-forties. That would be the pool I'd be fishing in for companionship if I was single and none of them appealed to me. They were all old ladies. Granted that Sandi was forty-four, but she looked like she was in her mid-thirties and as Barry had said – she was hot!

Could a single guy of forty-five attract younger good looking girls? I didn't think so. I was fit, had all my hair and teeth and Doris my secretary was always telling me that she would leave her husband and run off with me in a heartbeat, but I knew that was just office flirting.

She was in love with her husband and you couldn't separate her from him and her three kids with dynamite.

I realized I was wasting my time thinking of what to do. I knew me and I knew that what I was going to do was go straight at it and let the chips fall where they may.

***

After landing in Denver I stopped by the office and dropped off the paperwork and received congratulations from my boss. He asked me if I'd picked out my PA yet and I told him no and that I was having a hard time narrowing the list down. He laughed and said:

"Do what I did. I put all their names in a hat and drew one out. Patty has been with me ever since and I haven't regretted it at all."

I thought about for a second or so and then said, "I'll do that. I'll give you the name tomorrow."

And then I headed on home for the confrontation with Sandi.

I got home an hour before she did and I fortified myself with a couple of Jacks backed by water. I was sitting at the kitchen table when Sandi came in. She smiled, came over to me, bent and kissed me and then asked:

"How was the trip?"

"Fruitful. I signed the deal with Apex and starting tomorrow I move into the regional director's office."

"I'm glad for you, honey. I know how hard you've worked. What's next?"

"I have to pick a personal assistant from a group of six. They all seem well qualified and I'm having trouble deciding. You're a PA; what should I be looking for? One good at giving head? One who takes it in the ass and likes to do gangbangs?"

Sandi's face lost its color and her voice turned cold as she said, "What kind of question is that to be asking me?"

"Just wanted your opinion of what I should look for. I mean what with you being a PA and experienced in all that."

"What the hell do you mean by that, Robert?!"

"I had dinner with an old friend while I was in Chicago. Barry Watson. Name ring a bell?"

"No. Should it?"

"I would think so. It would seem reasonable to me that you would at least know the names of the men you fuck."

"This is not funny, Robert."

"I know. I didn't feel much like laughing either when Barry told me about the Dale and Sandi from Martin Industries that came to town to get Barry's company to sign a deal. Remember Cal and John or did you not learn their names either?"

"I have no idea what you are talking about, Robert, and I'm not at all pleased at what you are implying."

"Come off it, Sandi; you are busted. Unless you can somehow prove to me that there is another Dale who works for Martin and who also has a PA named Sandi and who was in Chicago three months ago to sign a deal with Amalgamated Machinery, you are toast. Barry even remembered your little idiosyncrasy; you know the one, telling everyone you are introduced to that it is Sandi with an i? What I want to know is how long has it been going on? How long have you been Martin's corporate whore?"

She must have finally realized that the jig was up and she sat down across from me. Actually it was more like she collapsed onto the chair across from me.

"I am not a corporate whore. Yes I did do those things with the men from Amalgamated, but it was not done to get them to sign anything. They had already agreed to sign and we were out celebrating and things got out of hand."

"So you are telling me never before or since?"

She looked away and said, "Not exactly."

"What the hell does not exactly mean?"

"I've been having kind of an affair with Dale since then."

"Kind of an affair? Just what the hell does that mean?"

"I've been seeing him off and on since we got back from Chicago."

"Well, ain't that just ducky. I've been getting sloppy seconds from my wife for three months now. Un-fucking real," I said as I got up from my chair and walked out of the kitchen and went out into the garage to work on my current project. A 1993 Mustang convertible with a 5.0 and a five speed. It had been wrecked and I got it for a song. It needed both front fenders, a hood and a front clip and even before the accident it hadn't been well cared for. The white leather seats were cracked and the top was in bad shape. I'd found the fenders on craigslist, but was still looking for a hood and a front clip.

I was bolting the right fender on when Sandi came out. She leaned on the door jamb and asked:

"What are you going to do?"

"I don't know yet. Divorce is a sure thing, but I'm undecided on the rest."

"The rest?"

"Do I sue Martin for letting one of its managers have sexual relations with a subordinate? Do I sue Dale for alienation of affections? If I sued the company you would probably both be fired. If I don't sue Martin, but go after Dale it would soon be common knowledge and you might still end up getting fired. Balance that against the fact that our salaries are pretty close to being equal and if you still had the job I shouldn't have to pay alimony. Like I said, I'm undecided."

"Does divorce have to be a sure thing?"

"What? I'm supposed to say I don't mind you gangbanging customers? I'm supposed to go see Dale and thank him for making me a cuckold? Of course there is going to be a divorce."

"It wasn't like that. I didn't set out to do anything. I thought I was safe with Dale. I've been with him for ten years and he has never once made a pass at me so I trusted him. I thought he had my back so I partied more than I should have, got carried away and taken advantage of. I won't lie to you. Once they got me going I got into it and they did things to me that I never even imagined doing. The next day I was ashamed of what I'd done and when the guys wanted to resume I told them to go to hell. Then Cal showed me the cell phone pictures he had taken and told me that I was going to party some more or the photos would be made public. I couldn't have that so I partied."

"So there are photos of it out there hanging over your head?"

"No. At least I don't think so. When it was over Cal handed me his cell phone and told me to delete them. He may have downloaded them, but I don't think he did."

"I'm having a hard time believing that you could do what Barry said you did and as easily as you did unless you had done things like that before."

"I had never done it before and that's the God's honest truth. We had spent a day and a half with the guys from Amalgamated trying to convince them to sign with us. When they did Dale said we would have dinner and a couple of drinks to celebrate. He invited the three from Amalgamated to join us and they did. We were going to a restaurant on the other side of town and since neither Dale nor I will drive when we have been drinking Dale set us up with a limo.

"We drove over to the restaurant and then talked as we had dinner. I wasn't paying attention all that close and the guys kept my wine glass full and you know what a large amount of wine will do to me."

Indeed I did. Wine loosened Sandi up and made her horny as all get out.

"I didn't think anything of it because as I said earlier I thought that Dale had my back. We finished dinner and Cal said that there was a place just a couple of miles up the road that had a pretty good band and it seemed like a good night to have a few drinks and do some dancing because we were celebrating right? Dale said it sounded good to him and we all got in the limo and drove to the bar. The band was good and Cal asked me to dance. After Cal there was John, Barry and finally Dale. My wine glass was kept full and I was having a good time.

"Maybe half an hour after we began dancing the guys began to get a little 'touchy-feely' with me and by then the wine had me real loose and so I giggled and let it go. When I didn't fight them off they got bolder and started playing with my ass and tits. I was horny, but I didn't think much about it because when I travel I always take my vibrating dildo with me and I knew I could take care of myself when I got back to my room. Again, I was expecting Dale to look out for me so I let things ride.

"It went on until last call and then we all got in the limo for the trip back to the hotel. I was on the one seat with John on one side of me and Cal on the other. Dale and Barry sat on the seat opposite. As soon as the limo pulled out of the bar parking lot Cal put his arms around me and kissed me. The way he had his arms around me immobilized my arms and I couldn't push him away and I couldn't push John's hands away when he started playing with my tits. Barry moved in front of me, pushed my legs apart and pushed his fingers in my pussy.

"I was already hot and horny from what had taken place in the club and when Barry's fingers pushed into me and started rubbing my clit I moaned and he pulled his fingers out of me, pushed my panties to the side and pushed his cock into me. Three strokes and I just gave it up. After that it was pretty much as you would expect. Barry fucked me while John sucked my tits and Cal pulled his mouth off mine and then shoved his cock in it. Barry finished, John took his place. John came and Cal took his place while Barry pushed his cock into my mouth. After that it was all repetition as the three of them used me over and over. Dale just sat there and watched.

"Cal told Dale we could have signed a lot sooner if I had been made available sooner. Dale laughed and said if he would have known I'd do it he would have offered me sooner. I was naked and Barry was fucking me when we got to the hotel so Cal told the driver to pull to the back of the parking lot until Barry could finish. When Barry came he had me right on the edge of an orgasm and when he pulled out I begged him to finish me. Cal told me not to worry and that they wouldn't leave me hanging. I had my eyes closed and was trying to push the climax when a cock was shoved in me. It caused me to explode and when I opened my eyes I saw that it was the limo driver who was fucking me. He fucked me hard and got me off once more before he got off and then they dressed me as we pulled out and drove up in front of the hotel.

"Dale and I got out and walked to the elevators and then we took the elevator up to our floor. Dale and I hadn't said one word to each other from the limo to our floor and when we came to Dale's room he grabbed my arm, unlocked his door and pulled me into his room. He took me in his arms, told me that he had always wanted me and then he kissed me. I had been on a sexual high for almost three hours and I was still up and when he gave me tongue I gave tongue back and then he took me to bed. He fucked me three times and then we fell asleep. When we woke up in the morning he fucked me again and then we dressed, had breakfast and went over to Amalgamated to finish up the paperwork, set delivery schedules and the like.

"While we were there Cal told me how much he had enjoyed the previous night and was looking forward to a repeat performance that night. I said no way. I told him that they had gotten me drunk and had taken advantage of me and it was not going to happen again. He laughed and told me that I had loved it and was one hundred percent into it and that we were going to do it again if I didn't want you to see what he had on his phone. One look at them and I knew I could never chance letting you see those photos, especially not the ones of me and the limo driver."

"Why? What was so bad about those?"

"He was black. He was black and you are a closet racist. You can deny it, but I know the tone of your voice and see the look on your face when you see…. Never mind, it isn't important. I gave in and that night was a repeat of the previous night except that we used a bed instead of a limo seat. Dale and the three from Amalgamated spent almost the entire night fucking me. Except for what has happened with Dale since that trip to Chicago the Chicago trip is the only time I have ever been unfaithful to you. I am not Martin's corporate whore and have never been."

"But by your own admission you have been cheating on me with Dale ever since that trip to Chicago."

"I know and I'm sorry that you had to find out."

"Why the affair with Dale? You went ten years working with him and if you are to be believed you never had any sort of sexual relationship with him. I can somewhat understand the night of your gangbang, but why since?"

"You already hate me enough that you are going to divorce me so I see no need to go into it."

"You might not see the need, but I do. You owe it to me to tell me how I failed you."

"How you failed? You never failed me, Bob. I'm the one who failed you."

"I had to have failed you somewhere along the line or you wouldn't be fucking Dale. I can see how Chicago happened and if you had come home to me and confessed and told me the story we could have possibly worked our way past it, but a three-month affair with Dale since then? I must have failed you in some area. You don't just go off and cheat on your partner for no reason. I want to know, Sandi. I have to know."

She looked at me steadily for about ten seconds or so and then she said:

"You never failed me, Bob; I failed you. You have always wanted to try anal sex and I have always refused. I always said that it was dirty, disgusting and I would never do it. That second night they took my ass, Bob. They didn't ask; they just took it. I was on my hands and knees and Cal was fucking me doggie while I was sucking on John. It was over an hour into the sex session and I was flying. I'd had a dozen orgasms and I was hot and into it. I was so into it that when Cal started used his thumb and fingers on my butt hole I barely noticed. It wasn't until he pulled his cock out of my pussy and put it at my butt hole that I noticed. I started to pull my mouth off John and tell Cal no, but at that point John was coming and he grabbed my head to hold it while he pumped his load down my throat and while I was gulping Cal pushed his cock into my ass and started fucking it. By the time John let go of my head what Cal was doing didn't feel half bad and by the time Cal came I was pushing back at him. I discovered that I loved anal sex. I almost prefer it to vaginal sex and I'm sorry as hell that I never let you do it to me. The problem was that I couldn't come home and say:

"Guess what. I found out that I love anal sex.

"All I could do was wait until you brought it up again and then pretend to reluctantly give in and then suddenly discover that it wasn't bad at all.

"It was an uncomfortable flight back home. Both Dale and I knew we had crossed a line and even though we had adjoining seats we didn't talk. When we got home I took three days off and considered resigning, but then said to hell with it. It was a one time thing and it would never happen again. Not only that, but you would never know.

"I went back to work and my working relationship with Dale was a little cool at first, but by the end of the week we were back on track. It was the Tuesday of the following week that everything changed. Dale and I had a working lunch with some people from the ad agency and I'd had a couple glasses of wine. Not enough to cause me to do anything like I had in Chicago, but enough to loosen me up. The people from the agency left and Dale said:

"I know that it is a sore subject for you, but I can't get Chicago off my mind. It was the most exciting and sexually satisfying thing that ever happened to me and I want to thank you for it."

"I couldn't believe it. He and Clara have been married for over thirty years and what we did was the most sexually satisfying thing he had ever done? I should have kept my mouth shut but I didn't. I said he had to be kidding me and he said no he wasn't. Clara had never let him have anal sex and the first he ever had was with me. It made him feel wicked and it excited him and he'd had one of the biggest climaxes of his life. I'd had enough wine in me that I told him I knew just how he felt. I told him it was the first time for me too. He told me that he couldn't believe it.

"That magnificent ass and Bob doesn't tap it?

"I told him that it was my fault and I told him why and that I was hoping and praying that you would bring it up again. Then he said that we should take care of each other until it happened. I said he was joking right and he said not in the least. He said all I had to do was give the word and he'd get up and get us a room. I thought back to that second night in Chicago and how I'd loved taking it in the ass and how it might be a while before I could get you to do it and then I told Dale to go get the room. Once in the room I made it absolutely clear to him that it would be anal sex only and even then only until I could find some way to get you into doing it with me."

"You are telling me that you only had anal sex with him?"

She looked away for a second or two and then said, "That was all it was supposed to be, but once I got into it other stuff happened."

"Other stuff?"

"Damn it, Bob! You already know the worst so why are you picking at the scab? Yes, other things! He got started, we both got off, but I needed more so I got him hard again. We both came again and I still wanted more so I got him up again and when he pushed me down on the bed and went for my pussy I didn't stop him. Since the first time it has been three quarters anal and a quarter of the others."

"How often?"

"Whenever he wanted. I didn't go after him, but I didn't say no when he asked."

"How often?"

"Some weeks once, some weeks twice and one week it was three times."

"That's a lot of sloppy seconds to be giving someone you say you love."

"You never, not ever, got sloppy seconds. I always showered, douched and brushed my teeth before leaving the hotel room. You may not believe me, but I do love you and I would never disrespect you like that."

"Bullshit, Sandi! Every time you were with him you were disrespecting me. Every time you brought your soiled body home to me after being with him you were disrespecting me."

"Now it is my turn to say bullshit, Bob! I love you and you know I do. I've shown it every day that we have been together. I fucked up and I admit it, but not once did I ever give my affections to another and before you even say it, sex for the sake of sex is not affection. And it cost you nothing, honey. What he got during the day was something you wouldn't have gotten anyway because you were working. If anything you came out ahead on the deal because I was still horny when I got home and I went after you."

"Yeah, and gave me sloppy seconds."

"I told you I alwa......"

"But I was still the second man in you that day. You may not have been sloppy, but I was still getting leftovers. Warmed up maybe, but still Dale's leftovers."

"I don't want a divorce, honey. I may be flawed, but I'm still yours, heart, body and soul. Please don't let my being weak ruin what we have had for over twenty years. I'll do anything, Bob; anything at all to stay your wife."

"I don't know, Sandi. You are asking a lot from me and I don't know that I can give it. You let me down, Sandi, and I don't know that I can trust you never to do it again."

"I swear, Bob, never again."

"Yeah, Sandi; you say that now, but how am I supposed to know that you mean it? The trust is gone, Sandi, and it will never come back. You have planted the seeds of distrust in my mind and those seeds are going to sit there forever. Even if I were to somehow convince myself to stay with you those seeds will keep reminding me of what you did. The weekend in Chicago isn't the killer, Sandi; it is the three months with Dale since that weekend.

"I'm going to trust that you never brought Dale into this house and into our bed so I'm not going to do anything drastic like burn the bed, but I am going to be sleeping in it alone. You need to move your things into one of the spare bedrooms until I decide what I'm going to do."

"Please, Bob; don't do this. Let me prove to you that I love you and want to stay with you. Let me make it up to you."

"How? By giving me Dale's ass? And it is Dale's ass since you gave it to him, but never to me. Just move your stuff, Sandi, and try to stay out of my way for a while."

I got up and left the garage as she started crying. I had to do it. I had to leave. To see the woman I loved crying made me want to take her in my arms and comfort her, but I couldn't. I had to stay strong and so I left.

***

I had one of the bedrooms set up as a combination home office and den. Sandi referred to it as my man cave and I went into it and closed the door. I sat down at the computer, brought up 'favorites' and clicked on 'accounts.' I selected the bank and checked on our accounts. There were four of them and one of them Sandi had no access to so I left the bare minimum in the other three and moved the majority of the funds into the account Sandi couldn't use. I did not believe that I could hang on with Sandi and I knew her well enough to know what she was likely to do if she thought for sure that I was going to kick her to the curb. I'd do the credit cards in the morning. Then I reconsidered my movements and transferred enough back into the joint checking account to cover the monthly bills.

When I was done I sat there and stared at the screen saver as I thought about what Sandi had done. It amazed me that she thought she could do what she did and that I would accept it and forgive her for it. If I had so much as kissed another woman under the mistletoe at a Christmas party I would have been living in a deep freeze and exercising my right hand for months, but I was supposed to accept the fact that she'd had a three month long affair? Again, if she had told me about Chicago we could probably have worked by it, but an affair? Jesus, what a fucking mess.

I killed another half hour in the den and then went out into the kitchen and made myself a bite to eat. Sandi wasn't downstairs so I assumed that she was upstairs moving her things. I watched some TV and around nine I headed up to bed. Sandi was sitting on the bed and when I walked into the room she said:

"Please, Bob, don't make me leave."

"Leave, Sandi. Don't make me pick you up and carry to your new room."

"At least I'd have your arms around me."

"How about I just grab a handful of your hair and drag you? Get the fuck out of here, Sandi, and stay away from me. If you need to be held, give Dale a call. After all, he is the one who has been seeing to your needs."

She got up and left the room crying. I didn't sleep all that well that night.

Chapter 2

The next morning I was up and gone before Sandi got up. I had breakfast at a coffee shop just up the street from work and when I got to the office I did just what Frank had suggested. I put the names of all six women on my PA list in a small box, shook it up and then reached inside and pulled out a name.

Pauline French was going to be my new personal assistant. Were the Gods fucking with me? Pauline is the only one of all the women on my list that I had lustful thoughts about. I imagined myself telling her that my wife was also a PA and then telling Pauline about how my wife took care of Dale and then telling Pauline that I wanted the same kind of PA. Then I saw myself in a sexual harassment suit and the thought faded fast.

Frank looked in on me and I told him that I had taken his advice and had pulled Pauline's name out of the box and that I'd offer her the position when she came in. He laughed and said:

"Keep it clean, Bob. I've seen the way you look at her south side when she's walking north and what's more I've seen the way she looks at you when she thinks no one is watching."

"You can't be serious."

"Just keep it clean, buddy. I'd hate to lose you over a bit of tail."

He left for his office leaving me with the thought "Pauline has been checking me out?"

Wanting to keep everybody as happy as possible under the circumstances I called all six women who had applied for the PA position into my office and then explained to them that they were all well qualified and so much so that I was having a hard time picking one of them. I told them what Frank's solution to a similar problem had been and that I had decided to do the same. I put a deck of cards and a box on my desk and said:

"I've put all your names into the box and to be fair I'm going to let one of you make the decision for me. High card will draw a name from the box and that will be the person I offer the position to."

Ann Marie was high with the ten of spades and she reached in the box and pulled out a slip. She went to hand it to me, but I told her to read it out loud. She did and while all the girls were congratulating Pauline and no one was looking I put the box with the slips that all had Pauline's name on them on the floor and put the box that had all the names but Pauline's on the desk in case anyone wanted to take a look. After everyone had congratulated Pauline and had gone back to work Pauline sat down across from me and said:

"You seem to have overlooked something?"

"What is that?"

"You didn't offer me the position and give me a chance to say yes or no."

"You are right; I never thought of that, but to be fair to me you did apply for the job so why would I think I needed to offer it to you? You don't want it?"

"I did when I applied, but I didn't know about your wife at the time."

"Sandi? What does she have to do with this?"

"Maybe nothing, I don't know and that is what I guess we need to talk about."

"You have my interest, Pauline. Just what do we need to talk about?"

"You had no way of knowing, but my sister works at Martin in the same department as your wife and her boss Dale. Pat, that's my sister, told me about three months ago that your wife and her boss were getting it on. She found out by accident. She was in the supply room getting a ream of paper for the copy machine and the supply room shares a rather thin wall with the men's bathroom and she overheard your wife's boss telling two other guys about the visit to Amalgamated and how your wife took care of the guys from Amalgamated and clinched the deal.

"One of the guys he was talking to asked if your wife was as hot as she looked and her boss said she was even hotter than she looked and then said that since she had done a gangbang in Chicago and had loved it maybe he could set up another one for them and they both said to count them in. This made Pat curious and she started watching your wife and her boss. She said they took a lot of long lunches together and a lot of times your wife came back from them with what Pat called a 'just fucked' look about her.

"One time when everyone was at lunch Pat came back early and had been walking by your wife's boss's office just as she heard:

"Oh God, but I do love this tight ass of yours."

Pat went and sat down where she could keep an eye on the door of the office and about twenty minutes later your wife came out with that 'just fucked' look that Pat had mentioned."

"So what does that have to do with me offering you the PA position?"

"I'm wondering if you are expecting me to be the same kind of personal assistant that your wife is?"

"God Lord no! Absolutely not! What my wife did destroyed our marriage. Why would I want that with you?"

"That's too bad."

"Why?"

"Because that's the kind of PA that I want to be."

"You can't be serious?"

"Of course I am. I've wanted you since the day I hired in and first saw you. I've fantasized being bent over your desk like your wife was probably bent over her boss's. When the position as your PA opened up I couldn't wait to apply. I imagined us on business trips and being in rooms with connecting doors that I would come through to you when our day was over. I saw myself sealing deals for you so you would get raises and promotions and become even more important to the company. I saw myself doing whatever it took to make my man need me enough to keep me around."

"Your man?"

"Yes, my man. I saw myself taking you away from your wife and then showing you that I would do anything for you. Absolutely anything!"

"You can't mean that."

"Oh but I do. I want you so bad I'll do whatever you want. Do gangbangs and pull trains to get you the deal? Done! Fuck the president and CEO of the company to get you promoted? Done! I'm yours to do with what you will. I'll fuck the world for you if you want me to, or I'll stay at home and raise your babies and no other man will ever touch me if that's what you want."

"I don't know what to say, Pauline. No, that's not true. I do know what to say about part of it. If I have to provide sex to get a signature on a contact it will never happen and the customer can stick the contract up his ass. The same goes for providing sex for promotions or raises. I'll resign before that ever happens."

"Okay then; that leaves bent over your desk, connecting doors on trips together or staying at home and having your babies."

"None of that is going to happen, Pauline. I'm a married man and until I'm not I won't cheat on my wife even though she has cheated on me. That's just the way I am."

"I know. That's just one of the reasons why I want you."

"That just doesn't compute, Pauline. On the one hand you want me because I won't screw around on a wife who screwed around on me and on the other you say you will be a promiscuous slut."

"You didn't listen to me. I said I would do anything for my man. That was the key. My man. My man would be my life and I would do whatever he wanted. From being a saint to being a slut. I give myself to my man. Totally!"

"Well I can't be your man while I'm married to Sandi." I paused and then said, "And besides, I don't know you well enough to consider you as a replacement for Sandi."

"Then why do you stare at my ass and legs every chance you get?"

"I didn't say I didn't lust for you, just that I don't know you very well."

"You will know me well enough by the time your divorce is final."

"You are assuming that Sandi and I won't work it out."

"Not likely and for the same reason you previously mentioned."

"Previously mentioned?"

"You won't cheat on a wife who cheated on you. A man with a moral code like that won't stay with a woman who stabbed him in the back."

I had no answer for that so I said, "I'm offering you the personal assistant's position, Ms. French. Please let me know your decision as soon as possible."

"You know I'm going to take it. I need to be as close to you as possible if I am going to have any chance at getting what I want."

"Okay then; your first job will be to get me a new secretary. Doris has given me two weeks' notice. Her husband has taken a job in Boston. Get with Doris and she can give you a feel for what my secretary needs to be like. I require more of a secretary than she be able to answer a phone and type."

"You do know that any secretary I pick for you is going to be ugly as sin, right? I'm not going to allow anyone that even remotely looks like competition to get close to you."

"Just don't get her too ugly. I do need to deal with her on a daily basis without my stomach becoming queasy."

We spent an hour gong over what her duties would be and what I'd be expecting from her. Then I began the process of moving out of my office and into the office that Dan Harvest, the previous regional director, had vacated when he retired. A small office with a connecting door was next to it and that is where Marsha Loomis, his PA, had worked. When Dan retired he took Marsha with him and they were married a week later.

Pauline wasted no time in telling me that Dan and Marsha had set the precedent.

"What precedent?"

"That the regional director marries his PA."

"Good Lord, woman; am I going to have to put up with this daily?"

"Yep. I have to make sure that you understand just how serious I am."

I shrugged. What the hell! What red-blooded man wouldn't like to have a woman like Pauline after him? But that was something that was going to have to wait. Living in a no-fault state I already knew from hearing the horror stories of friends who had gone through divorces just what I could expect when I went for mine. It might not be quite as bad for me since we didn't have children and Sandi actually did make about the same as I did so alimony shouldn't be much as long as I stayed calm and didn't go after Dale or his employer.

I would have to talk with Frank about possibly making me an 'acting regional director' and hold off on any increase in pay until after the divorce was final and then give me the difference between my old pay and my new pay as a bonus once I was a free man. The last thing I did before leaving the office was call an attorney and make an appointment.

***

On the drive home I thought about what Pauline had told me and I wondered if I was up to being 'her man.' There was a fifteen year age difference between us and that thought prompted another thought. What the hell did a twenty-seven-year-old fox see in a forty-five-year-old man? Well it did answer an earlier question that I had asked myself. I had asked myself if a forty-five-year old single guy could attract younger women.

Sandi was home when I got there and she had dinner on. I grabbed a beer out of the fridge as she said:

"Now that you have had time to think on it, do you still intend to go for a divorce?"

"Of course I am."

"But why, Bob? Okay so I slipped up and did a stupid thing, but I love you and you know I do. Why throw away twenty-three good years? We are good together, Bob, and we always have been. We don't need a divorce, honey. We can get past it; just give me a chance."

"No, Sandi; we might, just might, have been able to get by it if you had come to me and told me about the Chicago business, but there is no way I can get by the three months that you have been giving it up to Dale. It is a done deal, Sandi. I have an appointment to see an attorney tomorrow afternoon and you will probably be served with the papers by the end of the week."

"I don't want a divorce, Bob, and I'll fight it."

"Go ahead and fight, Sandi. All it will get you is debt. You can stall it; slow it down some, but you can't stop it. We live in a state where no fault divorce is the law. I file and it happens. I don't even have to give a reason. I file and sooner or later it happens. Under no-fault we split everything fifty fifty. The house gets sold and we each get half of the proceeds and we each get half of all the other assets. I file and you don't fight and you will get enough money out of the deal to set yourself up in a condo and have some cash to fall back on. You fight it and you will be paying an attorney who can't do anything but slow the process down. Nothing he can do can make me stay married to you. I've made up my mind not to go after your company or go after Dale because as long as you are working I won't have to pay alimony."

When I said that I could see the sudden thought cross her face and I cut it off at the pass.

"You can quit thinking that I'll keep you rather than pay alimony, but that won't work. What will happen if you quit your job or fight the divorce is that I'll either sue Dale and your company and use that money to pay the alimony or I'll drop the divorce, move out and stop paying the bills. The phone, gas and electricity will get turned off and since I won't be making house payments the house will go into foreclosure. You lose either way. Face up to it, Sandi; you have thrown your marriage away. Right now you need to be thinking of how to come out of it with something. That's the choice you have to make, Sandi. Come out of it with something or come out of it with nothing, but either way, Sandi, I'm gone."

Sandi started crying and left the room. I shrugged, got a plate and sat down to eat. When I was done I went out into the garage and worked on my Mustang.

***

The next day I talked with Frank and he agreed to what I wanted pay-wise. As long as I didn't take the raise in pay until after the divorce, Sandi and I would be making the same money.

Pauline was looking pretty good that day and I began thinking that I might have to change my mind on not having anything to do with her until my divorce was final. I'd begun thinking that once I filed and Sandi was served the marriage was as good as over and I should be free to play with Pauline.

That afternoon the attorney told me what I already knew and I told him to go ahead and prepare the papers and then have them served on Sandi Saturday morning when she would be at home.

When I left the lawyer's office I figured that there was no sense in going back to work for just an hour so I hit a Starbucks and went through the daily paper looking for an apartment to rent. I found and circled a couple and noticed that I had to go right by them on my way home so I decided to stop and check them out.

They were nice. Both had swimming pools, but one of them also had an exercise room, a steam room and a large hot tub. It was fifty bucks more a month than the other place, but to me it would be worth it. I signed up for a two bedroom unit, paid the requisite fees and headed for home.

As I drove I made a mental list of what I would need to furnish the place and I also made a mental note to find a storage place with a unit large enough to park the Mustang in and work on it.

Sandi was in the living room when I got home. She was reading a book and when I came in she looked up from it long enough to tell me that dinner was on the stove. I made myself a plate, ate and then went out to the garage to work on the car. At eight-thirty I went into the house and told Sandi that I needed to talk with her. We sat at the table in the kitchen and I told her that I had seen an attorney and that she would be served papers at the house on Saturday morning.

"You are going to do it? You are really going to do it?"

"Of course I am and I've already told you why. It will be a straight forward deal. Everything will be split fifty-fifty and our pay is about equal so there shouldn't be any alimony. We each keep our pensions and 401k's. The only thing that will need to be worked out is the house. If you want to keep it you can buy out my half otherwise it will be sold and we will split the proceeds equally."

"You don't want to buy out my half?"

"No. Too many memories. I don't want to live with constant reminders of what used to be."

"I think you are being foolish, Bob. I love you and you know I do. We can work it out. There does not have to be a divorce."

"I'm sorry, Sandi, but there is no way I can work by what you have been doing with Dale these last three months and you should know me well enough by now to realize that. I put a deposit down on an apartment today and I will probably move into it over the weekend. You need to decide what you want to do on the house. If you don't want it we need to get it listed."

I got up and headed for the bedroom. I took a shower and then lay in bed reading until my eyes got heavy and then I turned out the light and drifted off to sleep. Something tugging at my leg woke me up and when I opened my eyes I saw that the room light was on. I tried to sit up and couldn't because my arms were tied to the bed posts. I looked down and saw that the tugging on my leg was Sandi tying my legs to the bottom of the bed. I was tied spread-eagled on the bed.

Sandi was naked and when she saw I was awake she smiled at me and said:

"No need to panic. I don't want to hurt you. At least I don't think that it will hurt you. You do need to lay there and be quiet however since I really don't want to gag you if I don't need to."

"What the hell are you doing, Sandi?"

"All in good time, Bob. Just bear with me. I need to prep you first."

She climbed onto the bed and took my cock in her mouth. Even as upset and pissed off at her as I was there was no way my cock wasn't going to respond to her mouth and she had me up in no time. She worked on it for a while and then she got off the bed and went over to the dresser and came back with a tube of KY.

"I've already done me," she said, "I just need to get you ready."

She covered my cock with KY and then she got up on the bed and stood over me.

"This isn't the way I wanted it to happen," she said as she lowered herself down to me reverse cowgirl style. "But there is no way I'm not going to have you in my ass at least once."

She took hold of my cock, lined it up with her asshole and then pushed down so my cockhead pushed past her sphincter muscle. She took more of me in and then she fucked herself on my cock.

"Feel how tight it is, baby? You could have a steady diet of it if you wanted. Are you sure that you want a divorce? Would you really give this up when you don't have to?"

At that particular instant the answer was "Hell no I don't want to" but I knew that as soon as I got off and my cock went soft the decision to divorce was still going to be there.

"Cum for me, baby, let me have it; give it to me, baby, give it to me," she cried and I did. Sandi kept riding up and down until I started to go limp and then she got off me. She laughed and said, "Don't go away now" and she left me and went into the bathroom. She came back with a wash rag and a towel and cleaned my crotch area. She dropped the rag and towel on the floor and said:

"Now let's see what we can do with this limp thing here."

She started fondling my cock and I didn't say a word; I just watched. After a bit of fondling she took me in her mouth again and went to work. By then I realized she had no intention of hurting me so I just lay there and waited to see what was going to happen next. It goes without saying that my cock responded. Once she had it standing tall she climbed aboard cowgirl style and took me in her pussy. As she rode me she looked down at me and said:

"Are you sure you want a divorce, baby? You know I love you and I know you love this. Don't give it up, baby."

She got off me, turned to reverse cowgirl and took me in her ass again. As she moved up and down she kept telling me that I could have as much of her ass as I wanted and whenever I wanted.

"It's yours, baby; all of me is yours. I want you to take my ass doggie, baby. I want you to puppy fuck my ass."

She went up and came down hard and made the sounds that she makes when she orgasms and moaned:

"So good, so good; oh yeah, baby, so fucking good."

She kept going until I came and rode me until I started to soften and then she got off me and left the room.

She came back ten minutes later fully dressed and with a knife in her hands. I suddenly realized that my earlier thought that she had no intention of harming me might have been faulty and I guess it showed on my face as she said:

"Oh no, baby; I couldn't hurt you. I could never hurt you."

I watched as she untied my right arm and then dropped the knife where I could pick it up with my right hand.

"We'll talk tonight, baby," and she left. As I was cutting the rope tying my left arm to the bed I heard the garage door open and shortly thereafter close. I got myself loose, took a shower, dressed and then went to work.

***

As I drove I wondered what Sandi felt that we needed to talk about. I thought that I had made my position perfectly clear. Her dalliance with Dale had ended our marriage. That was cut and dried. The fact that my cock had finally been in her ass wasn't going to change a thing. I briefly considered pretending to drop the divorce and fucking Sandi's ass until she was served, but I quickly put that thought out of my mind. I couldn't be that much of an asshole. The idea was tempting and I could rationalize doing it as revenge for what she had done with Dale, but the bottom line was that I would still have to live with myself. I just wasn't the kind of guy who could do it and not feel guilty afterwards.

The day flew by at work and the only time I thought of being in Sandi's ass was when I saw Pauline's back side and wondered how tight it might be as I eased into it. And once again I thought of changing my stance on what my status would be when Sandi was served and I moved out. The marriage would be as good as over right? Technically, if not legally I would be single again right? And of course there was the fact that Sandi had broken her vows so that released me from mine right? Even as I had the thoughts I knew I was going to have my work cut out for me if I was going to overcome my basic programming as far as my marriage vows were concerned.

I had a surprise for Sandi. She had said that we would talk that night when we got home, but I wasn't going home. When I got off work I checked into a motel and then turned my cell phone off. I had dinner at the Outback Steak House and then stopped at Bud's Bar for a couple of beers before going back to the motel.

I had arranged with Frank to take the next day off so I slept late and then had breakfast at the IHOP next to the motel. After eating I called Martin and asked to speak to Sandi and was told that she was in a meeting. I was asked if I wanted to leave a message and I told the receptionist that I would call back later. Knowing that Sandi was at work and not at the house I headed to the U-Haul place and rented a truck and a car hauling trailer. By four I had everything out of the house that I wanted. I left my wedding ring in the middle of the kitchen table and then I left.

I drove over to my new apartment and moved in and then returned the truck and trailer. The U-Haul place also had storage units and I rented a large one and moved the Mustang, my tools and all my shop equipment into it. I hit a Denny's for dinner and then stopped at a Wal-Mart to buy some of the things I needed to set myself up in my bachelor pad.

I slept pretty soundly that night and when I woke up in the morning I realized that it was the first day of a fresh start. Even so it started on a sour note. I turned on my cell phone which had been off for thirty-six hours and it was full of missed messages and voice mails and they were all from Sandi. I deleted them all and debated cancelling the phone and getting a new one with a different number, but decided that it would be too much trouble given all the people I would have to contact and give the new number to. Half of whom would want to know why and I wasn't up to telling them.

***

When I got to work Doris was already there and she gave me a nasty look and said:

"You need to call your wife. She has called twenty-seven times since yesterday and she is accusing me of being a liar when I tell her that you are not here. She says that I'm just saying that because you told me to."

"I do not want to talk to her, Doris. I've moved out and want nothing to do with her anymore. When she calls put her on hold and leave her there until she drops off."

That prompted another thought and I went back down to the lobby and told the guard at the security desk that Sandi was under no condition to be allowed in the building. He shrugged and said:

"I'll put it in the log so the other shifts will see it, but I can't promise anything. When things get real busy here people can and have slipped by."

Knowing he was right I said nothing and went back to my office. Pauline came in and said:

"Why the sour look?"

I told her and she said, "Even if she gets by security, Doris and I will see that she doesn't get to you."

"How can you do that?"

"Stall her long enough for you to leave your office and go through mine to get to the back stairs."

"I guess I lucked out and got the right PA after all."

"And don't you forget it."

As she left the room and I watched her ass I wondered if she was wearing those tight slacks knowing what her marvelous ass was making me think? I slapped myself mentally. "Of course she knows you dummy."

At twelve I called Doris into the office and told her to get her purse as I was taking her to lunch as a way of thanking her for putting up with Sandi. Once we had given our orders Doris said:

"I'm not normally a nosy person, but I just have to ask. What's up with you and Sandi? I saw the two of you two weeks ago and you looked great together."

"That's because two weeks ago I didn't know what I now know. Sandi has been cheating on me for the last three months and I just found out about it."

"Sandi? Cheating on you? I find that hard to believe."

"This isn't a case of I think she is. I confronted her and she admitted it. She says that it was just a short fling and that we can get by it. I, on the other hand, don't see things that way."

"That's a shame. You and Sandi were so good together."

At that point our orders came. As we ate I asked her if Pauline had discussed with her what to do if Sandi showed up and she said that they had talked about it and that is what had prompted her question to me when we sat down.

"I'm butting in where it is none of my business, but I'd be careful where Pauline is concerned."

"Why would you say that?"

"When she was telling me what to do if Sandi showed up I could see that she was already thinking of how to take Sandi's place."

"Would that be bad? She is a damned good looking woman and smart too."

"Just be careful, Bob. Call it woman's tuition for lack of a better description, but I'm not sure that Pauline would be good for you. There is something about her that to me just doesn't ring right."

I changed the subject and asked what she planned to do when she got to Boston and that carried us through the rest of lunch. When we got back to the office I bit the bullet and called Sandi at work. When she answered I said:

"I'm not interrupting anything, am I? I mean I didn't catch you bent over Dale's desk or on your knees under it, did I?"

She hung up on me and I had to smile. She had been trying to get in touch with me and there I was on the phone and she hung up on me. I called back and told the receptionist that Sandi had been too busy to take my call so I'd leave a message for her.

"Please tell her to make sure that she is at home Saturday morning to take delivery of the package. If for some reason she can't be there I'll have it delivered to her at work on Monday. It is important, Cheri, so please make sure that she gets the message."

I left work early and hit the bank. In the papers that Sandi would be served with was a breakdown of the household expenses and she was informed that half of that amount was what she needed to set aside from her paycheck. Actually it was a good deal for her as she was living in the home while I was having to maintain a separate residence. Like the attorney said:

"You always lose something in a divorce no matter who is at fault."

I called and cancelled all of our joint credit cards and got the payoff balances of all of them. I cashed in two of the certificates of deposit that were in the safe deposit box and used the money to pay off the credit cards. That left five CDs, six U.S. Government savings bonds and some personal papers in the box so I rented another one in my name only and took three of the CDs and my personal papers – birth certificate, passport and the like – and moved them to the new box. That done I had the weekend to look forward to and I expected it to be busy with my settling into my new digs.

Saturday morning I got up and had breakfast at the IHOP and then hit a couple of stores to get more of what I needed to make apartment living more comfortable for me. That afternoon I hit the exercise room and was pleased to see several leotard clad lovelies there working out. I noticed that only one of them was wearing a wedding ring and I had the thought that the extra fifty bucks that the apartment was costing me was worth it just for the scenery. That thought was reinforced when I went to the swimming pool and saw all of the lovelies there. When I did start to play it looked like I had a 'target rich environment' to work with. Providing of course that Pauline didn't get me.

Once back in my apartment as I was making myself dinner it finally hit me. I was without Sandi in my life for the first time in twenty-three years. It was upsetting because I did love her. Not that I had loved her, but that I still did love her. I probably always would, but I just could not accept what she had done and put it behind me. I just wasn't wired that way. I knew I was going to miss her in the coming months, but there was no going back for me.

Chapter 3

Sunday was a day of getting used to my new life. I spent time in the exercise room and at the pool and I spent some time at the storage unit working on the Mustang.

Monday morning when I got to work Doris, who had already been there for a half hour, told me that Sandi had called three times in the past fifteen minutes. I decided to get it over with and I called her at work. The receptionist told me that she was in a meeting, but had left instructions that if I called Cheri was to interrupt the meeting and get her. Thirty seconds later Sandi was on the phone.

"You did it," she said. "You actually did it. How could you just throw away twenty-three years away?"

"Me? I didn't throw anything away, Sandi; it is all on you. Anyway, I am returning your three calls this morning. What do you want?"

"We need to sit down and talk, Bob. This is getting totally out of hand."

"There is nothing to talk about, Sandi. You did what you did and I cannot accept it."

"Okay, okay, I made a mistake. A big mistake, but it doesn't change the fact that we love each other. We can get by this, Bob. I know I'll have my work cut out for me, but we can do it. Just give me a chance, Bob."

"Why would I want to do that when by your own admission you were going to keep on stabbing me in the back for years and years to come?"

"I never said that!"

"Sure you did. You told me that you were letting Dale have your ass until you could get me to tap it. Do you deny that?"

"Well, no but…"

"No buts, Sandi. You have been giving Dale your ass for the last three months. In those three months did you do anything to start to ease me into thinking about trying to get you to let me have anal sex with you? No you didn't. You were going to keep fucking Dale until I made a move to try and have anal sex with you only I was never going to make that move. You said no to anal sex so many times that I came to accept that it never was going to happen and as a result I was never going to mention it again. That meant that you would keep on giving your ass to Dale for years and years to come.

"Barry told me that the boys were already making plans for the party they were going to have with you in nine months when you and Dale go back there to renegotiate the contract. And you would do it. After all, wouldn't you have been fucking Dale for a year and didn't you get into it the last time?"

"Damn it, Bob; I will never do anything like that ever again!"

"The problem, Sandi, is that I don't believe you. If I hadn't found out and confronted you about it you would still be fucking Dale several times a week. I've got an in at Martin and my mole tells me that Dale is trying to set you up for a gangbang with some of the other guys you work with and why would Dale do that if he didn't think you would go along with it?"

"Your mole is right. He has been after me to do it, but your mole should be telling you that I have absolutely refused to even consider it. It is not going to happen, Bob."

"That's what you say, Sandi, but again, I don't believe anything you say any more. The ease with which you have been cheating on me these last three months has me thinking that you have done it even before that Chicago trip."

"Damn it, Bob; I never ever did that!"

"How do you drive thoughts like that out of my mind given that I know what you have been doing? Those thoughts are there, Sandi, because your actions put them there and they will not go away. In fact, every time I see you or talk to you they come rushing back to the front of my mind. I'm sorry, Sandi, but I can't live like that. I can't spend my time wondering where you are or what you might be doing and who you might be doing it with. Again, the ease with which you have cheated on me since your Chicago trip is always going to be on my mind."

"I'll quit the job."

"Won't matter, Sandi. I'll still be working and since I can't be with you twenty-four hours a day seven days a week I'd always be wondering what you were doing when I wasn't around. Keep the job, Sandi. It pays well and it is more than you would get in alimony."

"I'm not going to give up, Bob. I love you and I know you love me and I know that we can work things out if you will just give me a chance."

"I do love you, Sandi, and I probably always will, but I can't live with you. I'm sorry, but I just can't. From now on all communication between us needs to go through my attorney. Goodbye, Sandi."

I hung up and I heard "Life sucks, doesn't it!" I looked over and saw Pauline standing in the doorway between her office and mine.

"Yes it does," I said, "but it still goes on."

"Can I offer to cheer you up? I make a pretty good meatloaf and I wouldn't mind company for dinner tonight."

I thought about it for a few seconds and then said, "Sure; why not. I'll bring the wine."

As soon as Pauline opened the door to her condo I saw that she was hoping for more than just a companion for dinner. Her blouse was cut low, her skirt was high and so were her heels. I did have to admit that she looked good enough to eat and I was sure that was the effect that she was aiming for.

She hadn't fibbed; she did indeed make a pretty good meat loaf. It was served with a baked potato, french style green beans and crusty sourdough bread. We washed it down with the Cabernet Sauvignon that I'd brought and then I helped her to do the dishes. As we left the kitchen for the living room Pauline said:

"I'm not a very subtle person, Bob. I have a tendency to go after what I want so I think you should know that there is nothing underneath what I'm wearing but skin. That should tell you what I'm hoping to have for dessert."

"That's a very tempting offer, but I'm still a married man."

"Bull crap boss man. You filed for divorce and I heard you on the phone telling her there wasn't a chance in hell that you would change your mind. To me that means that your marriage is over and therefore you are as good as single."

As she said that she was taking off her blouse and dropping her skirt on the floor. She stood there before me naked except for her high heels and as I feasted my eyes on her she said:

"You really want to turn this down?"

What the hell; I was only human. I was sitting there with a cock so hard you could have split bricks with it while the voices in my head argued. "You can't!" "Yes you can." "It isn't right; you are still married." "No I'm not. I've moved out and I'm moving on."

Pauline interrupted my thoughts. "Come on, Bob; you know you want to."

I stood up and she walked up to me and reached for my zipper and I stopped fighting it.

Pauline lived up to all that the package had promised. She was hot and she was damned near insatiable. She sucked me, I ate her, we made love, went sixty-nine and made love again. We showered together and I took her from behind as she leaned against the shower wall. As I was dressing she said:

"You don't have to go. I'd like to wake up next to you in the morning."

"If I don't leave now I wouldn't leave you alone and I wouldn't have enough energy left in me to drag myself into work in the morning."

"Get used to it, lover; it is going to be your steady diet from now on."

As I drove back to my apartment I wondered if I was physically able to handle a steady diet of what Pauline promised. I also wondered if I wanted to jump into a new long term relationship when I didn't even have the paperwork that would end my last one. I fell into an exhausted sleep when my head hit my pillow.

***

The next day Pauline was totally professional. No one seeing us together would have even thought that there was something going on between us. It wasn't until quitting time and after Doris had gone home that she asked:

"Are you stopping by tonight?"

"No, I don't think so."

I saw the disappointment in her eyes and I said, "I thought that since you cooked for me last night I would cook for you tonight."

Dessert at my place was every bit as exhausting as dessert at her place had been. The only difference was that she was still in my bed when the clock went off at six. Our morning shower had predictable results and we had to hurry in order to make it to work on time.

Every night for the next six weeks found me either at Pauline's place or Pauline at mine. At work everything was kept on a professional level and no one would suspect ever suspect up of being bad.

Sandi had stopped trying to get in touch with me and my attorney told me that she had gotten an attorney and was fighting the divorce.

"She can't stop it, but she can slow it down and make it expensive enough that you might decide to drop it."

"Let me think about it for a bit. I might be able to come up with something that will make her back off."

Just when I thought that life couldn't get any more complicated I got a phone call that proved me wrong. I was sitting in a booth at Duke's Steak House looking at the menu when I saw Pauline coming toward me. I wondered how she knew I was there, but then I noticed that she wasn't wearing the same clothes that she was wearing when I left the office. Since she didn't know that I was going to be here I concluded that she was meeting someone.

Wrong conclusion I thought as she headed right for me. She walked up to the table and I stood to greet her. Instead of just taking a seat she offered me her hand as she said:

"Hi. I'm Pat and I can tell from the look on your face that you didn't know that Paulie and I are twins."

"No, as a matter of fact I didn't know. Please sit down. What can I get you to drink?"

"A vodka tonic with a slice of lime would go good right about now."

The waitress was there as soon as Pat sat down and I ordered drinks for both Pat and myself. As soon as the waitress was gone I asked:

"So what is this really important thing that you need to talk to me about? All your phone call said was that it was important that you see me about Pauline."

"There is this thing about twins. They are either joined at the hip, know each other's thoughts and they live and act as one or they hate each other. Maybe not hate, but they don't get along all that well. Paulie and I fall into that second category. We didn't start out that way, but when we reached middle school things started going bad between us. Paulie started wanting what I had. Before we started middle school we shared. What was mine was hers and what was hers was mine.

"In middle school we discovered boys and for some reason if I had a boy Paulie just had to take him away from me. I never understood it because she could have had her pick of guys, but the ones she wanted were always the ones I had. In fact, if she had a boyfriend when I started seeing a guy she would drop her boyfriend and then start after my guy. She was always able to take them away from me because she would always give them something that I wouldn't. I wouldn't put out, but Pauline would and did. It went on all the way through junior high and high school and it only stopped after high school because we went to different colleges."

At that point our waitress arrived with our drinks and took our order. When she was gone I asked:

"What has that got to do with me?"

"I'm getting to that. I went to college here and Paulie went to college in Ohio so she wasn't around to intrude on my relationships. I met Brian and fell in love and it seemed that he loved me. I started planning my future with Brian. Paulie didn't know Brian and had never met him. When she came home on summer break between our sophomore and junior years he was back in Ohio working as an intern at his father's business.

"She finally met him during spring break in our junior year. Brian didn't go home for break and Paulie came home and they met. By that time Brian and I were already planning on being married the week after graduation. I didn't think anything at all about Paulie trying to take Brian away from me because Brian and I were in love and there was nothing Paulie could do about it. I should have been on my guard, but I wasn't.

"Paulie and I look alike, sound alike and act alike. If I hadn't told you I was Paulie's sister would you have known? I mean if I had just walked up and sat down and asked you to order me a drink would you have known I wasn't Paulie?"

I had to admit that I would not and then I asked for the second time what it had to do with me.

"Be patient with me for another couple of minutes. You have to know the story behind things before I let you know where you come in. It was a Tuesday night and I had a date with Brian to go to a play we wanted to see. I was running a little late getting home and I wasn't there when Brian got there. Paulie was and she pretended to be me and she and Brian left. They were gone when I got home and I hurriedly got ready for my date and then I waited and waited for Brian, but he never showed. I couldn't understand his standing me up. If something had come up surely he would have called. I went to bed pissed and I was asleep when Brian brought Paulie home.

"The next day when I asked him where he had been and why he hadn't at least called he asked me what in the hell I was talking about. That is when I found out what Paulie had done. I got into a big fight with Paulie over it and she said it was just a practical joke. I couldn't fault Brian over it because how could he have known?

"Things settled down and Paulie went back to school. Summer break came and Brian went back to Ohio to work in his father's business. Paulie didn't come home for the summer. She said she was taking summer classes so she could graduate early. A month into summer vacation I got to missing Brian really bad so I decided to go see him. I didn't call ahead because I wanted to surprise him. I was the one surprised. I caught Brian and Paulie together. To cut the story short Paulie put out for him on the date she stole from me. I had never put out for Brian because I intended walking down the aisle a virgin, but once he had a taste of Paulie he wanted more and he and Pauline managed to get it on a couple of more times over spring break. They picked up where they left off when Brian went back to Ohio for the summer.

"I'm afraid that I wasn't very lady-like when I caught them. I called Brian every name I could think on and I kicked him in the balls a couple of times, told him I hoped he rotted in hell and then came home. Blood being thicker than water and family being family Paulie and I eventually got back on speaking terms. She even told me that she was doing it for me and that she intended to tell me about it at the end of summer vacation. She told me that Brian knew that it wasn't me when he took her out on that date and that he went after her so that after we were married he would be able to say he had slept with twins. I never spoke to Brian again so I have no idea if that was true or not.

"That brings us to your question. What does any of it have to do with you? I promised myself that someday I would get even with Paulie. It has taken years, but I can finally stick it to her."

"Again, I fail to see where I enter in to this."

"Paulie has set her sights on you. She is already seeing herself as your next wife. My goal is to keep that from happening and even though Paulie is not aware of it she is helping me reach that goal."

At that point our order came and the talking stopped as we ate. As we ate I was thinking about what Pat had said. I was thinking of Pauline as a second wife and why wouldn't I? Great looking, a good cook. Fun to be with and marvelous in bed. Her apartment was always spotless and she certainly seemed to care for me. I had a hard time believing that Pat thought she could prevent Pauline and I from getting permanently together and an even harder time believing Pauline would help Pat reach her goal even inadvertently.

Gail and I both said no to dessert and I said, "Okay Pat, I know why you want to sabotage Pauline's relationship with me, but what makes you think you can do it?"

"I'll let Pauline do it for me."

She reached into her purse and brought out a mini-cassette recorder and set it on the table between us.

"Paulie conveniently forgets how she has been where I am concerned and when she visits and gets a few glasses of wine in her she gets very talkative and I listen. I know Paulie and how she is and once she told me about her plans for you I started to secretly tape our conversations. This one is from last Tuesday." She pushed the 'play' button.

"So how goes your seduction of your boss?"

"I've got him wrapped around my little finger," Pauline said and then she laughed. "Or maybe I should say I've got his cock wrapped with my pussy."

"Just what is so special about this guy?"

"He's got money, honey, and he is going to make a lot more now that he has been promoted and I can see a couple of more promotions in his future. I'm going to be on easy street, Pat. I'll be living the life I deserve."

"But do you love him?"

"Love smove; all that matters is that I like him enough to put up with him. He's not half bad in bed, but it doesn't matter. If I'm in the mood for a real fucking I've always got Randy to fall back on."

"You would cheat on him? Isn't that why he is divorcing his current wife?"

"I'm smarter than she was. The stupid cunt set herself up to be caught. Bob will never know about Randy."

"You would risk the good life you say you want just to screw an ex-boyfriend?"

"We are great together in bed. Why give up great sex if you don't have to?"

"So you are going to marry this guy for money and keep Randy around for sex."

"Yep. The best of both worlds."

Pat hit the stop button. "Maybe you think her pussy is worth living with the cheating she is going to be doing. Only you know that, but I can at least say that you were warned."

"I guess you can. I suppose I should thank you, but...oh damn! I had two girls cheat on me before I met Sandi and then Sandi and now this. What the hell do I have to do to get a woman who will stay faithful?"

"She's out there. You'll find her."

I looked at her and then smiled. "How much like your sister are you?"

"What do you mean?"

"I was thinking along the lines of a re-enactment. Pauline pretended to be you to snag Brian so you tell her you pretended to be her to hook me. Say we arrived at the restaurant at the same time. I was surprised to see Pauline and before you could tell me that you were her twin sister I said we should skip lunch and go to my place and have a nooner. You saw the chance to get even with her for what she did with Brian and you took it."

"It would be perfect except for one thing. I'm not like Paulie that way. I don't just jump into bed with guys."

"Not even to get back at Pauline?"

"Not even."

That isn't what I wanted to hear, but I wanted to stay on Pat's good side so I said, "Good."

"Good?"

"I'm not the kind of guy who can just jump into bed with a girl, but Pauline doesn't have to know that we didn't do anything. I'll take the rest of the afternoon off and when I go into work in the morning she will no doubt ask me where I was and I'll look at her astonished and tell her that she knows damned well where we were and then say something like "Was my performance in bed so bad that you've already forgotten it?" Whichever way the conversation goes Pauline will end up knowing that as far as I knew I'd spent the afternoon in bed with her – or someone who looked an awful lot like her. She's not stupid and she will figure it out and when she hits you with it all you have to do is say:

"Remember Brian? The scales are being balanced. I liked him and I'm going to do my best to see him some more."

"Just don't tell her about the recording. She is a pretty good PA and I want to keep her around. Also I'll let her keep my bed warm until she finally figures out that I'm not going to marry her."

"If you need a bed warmer why not let your wife do it? She would kill for the chance."

"How do you know that?"

"We have become friends since I told her what Dale had planned for her."

"What Dale had planned for her?"

"I know Paulie told you what I told her about overhearing what Dale, Jared and Tom talked about in the men's room. Well, after that every time I saw two or three of them go into the bathroom together I would go into the supply closet and listen to what they talked about. I heard Dale tell them he couldn't get your wife to do a gangbang and that your wife had cut him off. I heard both Jared and Tom tell Dale they had tried to get your wife to go out with then and she wouldn't.

"I heard Dale tell Jared that your wife told him to leave her alone and stop trying to get her to have sex with him or she would go to management and file sexual harassment charges against him and that Chicago would probably be brought up and they would both be out of work.

"The one that finally made me go to your wife was when Dale told Tom that the next time he had a working lunch with your wife he would slip her some date rape drugs, get her in a hotel room and then call Tom and Jared and they could have the gangbang they wanted. I went to your wife, told what I'd heard and since then we have become good friends.

"She knows what she did was wrong and she hates herself for it, but what is killing her is losing you. I know what she did and why and she did screw up big time, but are you a saint? Look back on your life and I'm sure that you will see times when you screwed the pooch big time and I'm sure that at those times someone had to forgive you. Why can't you find a little forgiveness in you?"

She looked at her watch and said, "I've got to get back to work." She opened her purse, took out a business card and handed it to me. "Call my cell and keep me up to date on what you tell Paulie so I can match your story when she jumps me over our 'afternoon dalliance'" and then she was gone leaving me with a headful of questions and no answers. I remembered what Doris had said about Pauline and I wondered what it was that she saw in Pauline that I had missed.

I caught the afternoon matinee at the Rialto to kill the afternoon and then I went home. When my cell chimed I looked at the display and saw that it was Pauline so I let it go to voice mail. She called me twice more in the next two hours and I took the second call. After I said hello she asked if I was home and when I said yes she asked if she could come over.

"You didn't get enough this afternoon?"

"Enough what?"

"Oh come on, Pauline; was my performance in bed so bad that you have forgotten about it already?"

"What are you talking about?"

"Skipping lunch and having a long afternoon in bed with you. What else would I be talking about?"

She was silent for a bit and then she said, "I just remembered that I promised my sister I'd stop by and see her tonight. See you in the morning okay? Bye."

As soon as I hung up I got out Pat's card and gave her a call. When she answered I said:

"Don't need to wait until tomorrow to talk to Pauline. She just called and wanted to know if she could come over" and then I told her how the conversation had gone. "If I'm right she is already on her way over to see you. Call me and let me know how things go."

"I'll do that. Bye."

I figured that I wouldn't hear from Pat until the next day so I watched some TV before going to bed. I was sitting up in bed reading Randy Wayne White's newest novel when my phone rang. I saw that it was Pat's number so I answered it. After my greeting she said:

"Paulie just left and she was fuming. Called me a treacherous bitch and I just laughed at her. Anyway, she came over like you thought and as soon as she was in the door she asked me where I had been that afternoon and I knew that she had figured it out. I told her the story you suggested and then said that it was so good that I was thinking of going after you myself. That's when she called me a treacherous bitch. I laughed at her and said:

"Remember Brian? I think this makes us even so now all you have to worry about is whether or not I'll settle for even or if I might want to get ahead."

"That's when she stormed out. Keep me up on what happens next okay?"

"You got it. Talk to you later."

I was smiling when I finished the chapter I was reading and then I turned off the night and went to sleep.

**

The next day at work Pauline was as professional as usual and just before quitting time she asked:

"Your place or mine?"

I thought of pulling her leg and telling her that I had something else going that night, but then decided not to push it. Pauline was good pussy and I saw no sense in messing up a good thing until I absolutely had to so I said:

"Your choice."

"My place then. I feel like cooking and I've always heard that the way to a man's heart is through his stomach."

"For some men maybe, but the way to mine is below my stomach and hangs down when it isn't sticking straight out."

"I'll try both routes then just to make sure I get where I want to go."

I just smiled and she told me that she would see me there. As she walked out of my office I watched her ass and thought that it was too damned bad that she was the way she was. If I hadn't heard the tape that Pat had made Pauline could have very well been my second wife. That thought caused me to think of my first wife and I thought about what Pat had told me. I made two decisions and both of them were going to cost me. One would cost me some money and one could cost me some time in jail, but I had to do them.

I got out the Yellow Pages and found what I was looking for and made an appointment for the next day and then I headed over to Pauline's to get fed and fucked. The next day Gavin Meyers of Spenser Investigations took my check and the information I'd given him and told me that I should hear from him in about two weeks.

The two weeks flew by and were fairly uneventful. I was spending the night with Pauline three or four nights a week either at my place or hers and we had sex almost every night and some times in the mornings. Half a dozen times during both weeks Pauline had me do her in her butt and I loved it. When Sandi had tied me to the bed and basically raped me I had loved the super tight feel of her ass and she had obviously liked my being in there. Pauline loved it too. She even had orgasms several times while I packed her fudge.

Two weeks to the day Gavin Meyers from Spenser Investigations called me and told me he had what I wanted. It was all there. The nights I hadn't been with Pauline she had spent with Randy McComb. I already knew about Randy from Pat, but I couldn't throw Randy in Pauline's face without her knowing that I got it from Pat so I had to have another source. I didn't intend to use it any time soon because as I had told Pat Pauline was a damned good PA and I was in no hurry to lose her. However I did see the time coming when I would have to use it.

The other information I got from Spenser would be put to immediate use. I called in some favors and then one night when Dale pulled into his driveway and got out of his car I was waiting and he never saw the first punch. It was not supposed to be a fair fight; it was supposed to be a beating so I didn't feel the least bit guilty about the sucker punch. I was wearing a ski mask so he couldn't see my face, but that wouldn't keep him from knowing who I was.

After that first punch I beat the shit out of him. He was lying on the ground and barely moving when I kicked him twice in the crotch. I bent down, grabbed a handful of his hair and pulled his face up to mine. With my face only inches from his I said:

"This is only a sample of what will happen to you the next time you lay a finger on Sandi. Put all thoughts of Sandi, date rape drugs and gangbangs out of your mind. If I hear that you have been anything but professional with her I'll see you again and you have my solemn promise that next time I'll put you in the intensive care unit at the hospital."

I let go of his hair, kicked him in the family jewels one more time and then I left. Did I worry about the police? Of course I did, but the favors I'd called in were from five guys who would swear that I had been playing poker with them all evening. Could the cops break the alibi? Possibly, if they tried hard enough, but I was gambling that they wouldn't try all that hard. Maybe if I had killed Dale, but just for a beating? I didn't think so. Also there was the fact that I was sure Dale recognized who his assailant was and that if the cops dug deep enough and hard enough that the reason for the beating would come out and I was pretty sure that he didn't want that. Like I said, it was a gamble.

After I left Dale's I drove over to the south side of town. It was a night that Pauline and I weren't going to get together and out of curiosity I drove past 1343 Windsong Lane and I saw that Pauline's car was parked in the driveway. Just for a second I thought it might be interesting to stop, ring the doorbell and ask if I could have a few words with Pauline, but I quickly shook off the thought and headed for home.

The next morning I called Pat and asked her to keep her ear to the ground for me over the next couple of days and she said she would and then asked me why. I just told her that there had been some recent developments that might make things in her department at Martin's interesting and that if I was right there would be no more talk about date rape drugs and gangbangs.

That afternoon my attorney called me and told me that Sandi's attorney had asked for a conference to discuss voluntary counseling and that if I wasn't willing he would petition the court to order counseling. I told him that no way was I going to agree to that and to put to bed the bullshit about court ordered counseling I would just go ahead and stop the divorce.

"Just pull the papers and send me your bill. When she finds some other guy and decides to get married again she can bring the divorce."

"I hate to say it, but that's probably your best move at this point."

The next morning I was just walking into my office after a ten o'clock meeting when the phone rang. Gwen, my new secretary answered it and said it was for me. I picked up and it was Pat.

"Dale came to work this morning with two black eyes, a split lip and walking with a limp. I put that and your phone call yesterday together and came up with what I believe is the right answer. Care to comment?"

"Nothing other than to say that it couldn't have happened to a more deserving guy."

"The story he is putting out is that he was mugged and his wallet was stolen."

That pretty much told me that my gamble had paid off and I wouldn't be having a visit from the police.

"Thanks for the call. Keep your eyes open okay?"

"I will. Take care. Bye-bye."

That afternoon just after three Gwen told me that I had a call on line two. I picked up the phone, said hello and heard Sandi say:

"You still care. I know you do so why won't you give me a chance?"

"Because I don't want to get burned again."

"You don't have to worry about that. You know that it isn't going to happen again."

"I knew it was something I was never going to have to worry about when we said our vows, but it still happened, didn't it?"

"I explained that, Bob. You have to know that I will never let it happen again."

"I've already told you, Sandi; we could have possibly have gotten by what happened in Chicago, but the three months after are the sticking point."

"I explained that too, Bob. There was no love or affection involved. It was just something to hold me while I tried to come up with a way to get you to try anal."

"I don't seem to recall any attempt on your part to get me to have anal sex with you, Sandi. Not once during the three months you were putting out for Dale do I remember you doing anything to even remotely suggest that you wanted me to try anal sex with you."

"I couldn't. If I would have you would have wondered why my sudden interest after always having said no. I had to wait for you to bring it up. Please, Bob, give me a chance. I know you still care. What you did to Dale proves that."

"What I did to Dale? I don't know what you are talking about."

"Bullshit, Bob. Deny it all you want, but I know it was you who beat him up. He has been walking on eggshells around me ever since he got to work this morning. I know you care so why won't you give me a chance?"

"I have to hang up now, Sandi. I have a meeting to go to. Goodbye."

I didn't have a meeting to go to, but I needed to end the conversation. The fact was that I did care. Actually the fact was that I still loved the woman, but I didn't think that I could live with her given her three month affair with Dale. I sat there staring at the phone as I wondered about what I'd just thought. I didn't 'think' that I could live with her, but did I 'know' that I couldn't? That prompted the thought "Why not give her the chance she wanted and see?" My thoughts were interrupted by Gwen telling me that Frank wanted to see me so I got up and headed for his office.

When I got back to my office it was almost quitting time and I asked Pauline if it would be her place or mine that night.

"Neither, sweetie. I promised my sister I'd stop by and visit her tonight."

I put a disappointed look on my face and she caught it and said, "I'll make it up to you tomorrow night, lover. Take your vitamins; it could be a long night for you."

On a hunch I went into the men's room, took out my cell and called Pat. As I expected she didn't know anything at all about a visit from her sister.

"I haven't talked to Paulie since the night she stormed out of my place."

That told me that Pauline was probably going to be spending the night at a condo on Windsong Lane.

I left work and headed for Bud's Bar for a brew or two and while I sat at the bar nursing a PBR and watching the Bronco's beating the Raiders I again wondered if Sandi and I could make a go of it. On a whim I left the bar and headed for the house. As I turned onto the street I saw Sandi getting into a car parked in front of the house. I saw her slide over and kiss the driver. Not a quick peck on the cheek, but a solid kiss. When the car drove away from the curb I decided to follow. Ten minutes later the car pulled into the parking lot at the Texas Roadhouse. Sandi and the driver sat in the car and necked for a couple of minutes and then she and the man got out of the car and, then hand in hand, they walked into the restaurant. Once out of the car I recognized the man. It was Bill Neubert. He had been Sandi's boyfriend from the seventh grade until their second year in college. They'd had a big fight and had broken up and a week after their breakup I'd asked Sandi for a date and we had been together ever since.

Curiosity got the best of me and so I waited until they came out and then I followed them back to the house. They both went inside and an hour later the inside lights went out and after an hour wait with no one coming out of the house I headed on back to my place. As I drove back to my apartment I thought of a couple of things and decided to go ahead and do them. The house still had my name on the mortgage so I had the legal right to do what I wanted to do.

In the morning I called Gavin at Spenser Investigations and told him what I needed and the next day, after making sure that Sandi was at work, I met a man from Spenser's and by noon the house was wired for audio and video. When I first saw my attorney he had informed me that without direct physical evidence of adultery I would be hard put to come out of the divorce without being on the losing end financially. All I had was Sandi's confession and she could always deny it if it was in her best interests.

If Sandi and Neubert were doing what I was certain they were doing I would have evidence that I could use if I reinstated the divorce. Sandi and I were still married and it would be evidence of adultery. I knew I was just as guilty, but I didn't know if Sandi even knew about

Pauline, but even if she did I doubted that she would put a private detective on me to gather evidence. Why would she? She wanted us back together. Curiously enough I was not angry or upset at what she was doing with Neubert. I realized she was a healthy female and had needs and I wasn't there to fulfill them. After all it was the same needs that were behind my taking up with Pauline. The difference between what she was doing with Neubert and what she had done with Dale is that while she was fucking around with Dale I had been there to meet her needs. It was no fault of mine that I hadn't been meeting her anal needs. That was strictly on her.

***

The next three weeks went by and once a week I would stop by the house while Sandi was at work and get the DVD out of the recorder hidden in the garage and put a fresh one in and then I'd get the tape out of the recorder on the phone line and put a new tape in. I'd watch the discs at my apartment while waiting for Pauline or on nights when Pauline and I didn't get together. Neubert wasn't there every night, but he did average twice a week.

It wasn't the sex I was paying attention to although at times I did get a charge out of watching Sandi fuck. She wasn't any different with Neubert than she had been with me, but I was seeing things I'd never been able to see when I was doing her. I'd never seen her facial expressions when I had been doing her doggie or reverse cowgirl. I'd never seen her feet when I made love to her so I never knew that the toes on her right foot curled downward and the toes on her left foot didn't.

What I got out of the discs was what was talked about. Neubert wanted her to let the divorce happen so he could marry her, but she kept telling him that the only man she wanted to be married to was me and that she would never consent to a divorce. She said she would fight to the death to keep it from happening.

"As long as we are married I have hope that he will come back."

"How can you make love to me if you feel that strongly about him?"

"I am not making love to you. I am a healthy woman and I need sex and I'm getting what I need from you. That's all it is, Bill; the sex I need. I only make love with my husband."

One of the things I heard that I couldn't understand was her position on anal sex where Neubert was concerned. He kept asking her to let him have her ass and she kept telling him that her ass was only for her husband. Why was she saying that when it was her desire to get butt fucked and her letting Dale do it that put us where we were?

At least once a week Pauline would ask me how my divorce was coming and I told her it was going slow because Sandi was fighting it and that she and her lawyer kept throwing up roadblocks.

Once a week I'd call Pat to see if she had picked up anything and she always said she hadn't.

"Your wife and Dale seem to be professional with each other and if they are doing anything it is away from here, but in my talks with her I get the impression that the only relationship she has with him is a working one. She tells me that you have stopped the divorce. Having second thoughts?"

"Maybe," I said and then wondered why I said it.

***

It was a Tuesday and Pauline wouldn't be over that night. Off 'visiting her sister' she said. I'd swung by the house and had picked up the latest from the recorder and I sat down and had a beer while I listened to the phone tape and watched the video. There was nothing on the phone tape – there never was – just normal calls and the occasional call from Neubert setting up a date. The video showed that Neubert had been there Sunday and I watched as they sucked and fucked and then it got interesting.

Neubert had Sandi on her hands and knees and was doing her doggie while he worked on her butt hole with his fingers. She kept telling him to stop, but she was pushing back at him and he mistook that to mean that she didn't really mean for him to stop. Even I, watching the video, knew that she was pushing back on the cock that was fucking her because that was what she always did when getting it doggie, but Neubert decided that it was his fingers in her ass that was making her respond that way.

He pulled out of Sandi's pussy, put his cock against her asshole and started to push. Sandi dropped flat on the bed, rolled onto her back and kicked Neubert square in the nuts.

"God damn you! I told you no! I've told you no all along and I've told you why. Get your ass dressed and get the hell out of here and don't bother calling me anymore."

It was kind of funny watching him dress while trying to hold onto his balls and as Sandi rained curses down on him. He left and when he was gone Sandi came back into the bedroom. She sat down on the bed, opened the bedside table, took out the framed photo of me that used to set on the table on her side of the bed and hugged it to her chest. And then she started crying.

I shut off the player and sat there staring at the blank screen. I must have sat there for five minutes or so as a thousand thoughts raced through my mind. I wasn't even aware that I'd picked up the phone and made the call until I heard Sandi's voice say "Hello?"

The End

Here is a sample from another story you may enjoy:

10 SEXY STORIES IN 1

Naughty Wives

JUST PLAIN BOB

EROTICA SHORT STORIES, VOL. 29

"How long has it been since you last had sex?"

The question caught me totally off guard. For the first time I noticed how Tanya was dressed. Low cut blouse that showed off her ample cleavage, short skirt and high heels that show-cased her marvelous legs and friend or no friend I couldn't help but get a hard on. Then I remembered Tom's "I'm a 100% on board" comment and I had an idea where things were going. In a subdued voice I told her that it had been a year and a half.

She leaned toward me and I got a look down inside her blouse as she huskily said:

"I'd like to change that, Rob."

"Tom's my friend, Tanya; I can't do that to him."

I started to get up, but she grabbed my arm and pulled me back down. "Tom's okay with this, Rob, that's why he left, to give us some time alone. This isn't a pity fuck or a mercy fuck, Rob. Tom and I have talked this over for months now. You have something we want so hopefully I can help you and you can help us."

"I don't understand what you are saying."

"To be blunt about it, Rob, Tom is sterile and we want a child. We want you to give me one."

I was stunned! I sat there and stared at her speechless. When I finally did find my voice I said:

"You just said that you knew I wouldn't cheat on Peg."

"Yes," she said as she laid a hand on the lump in my trousers, "but that was before you knew what Peg was doing. Now that you know, you are released from your vows to her."

"Why me?"

"We want it to be someone we know and not some anonymous sperm donor. We are also going to want you to be part of the child's life. You will be the godfather and will always be around as Uncle Rob."

"This doesn't make any sense, Tanya."

"Of course it does. What if something happens to Tom and me? Who better to take care of the child than Uncle Rob? On the bad side, God forbid, what if the child needed a liver transplant or something like that. Could we find the anonymous sperm donor? And even if we did, would he help? If we got on a waiting list how long would we have to wait to find a donor who would be a match? No Rob, we've thought it through; we want you to be a part of our family. On the other side of the coin, are you going to tell me that you don't find me sexy?"

She squeezed the hard lump in my trousers and said, "This says you do" and then she dropped to her knees in front of me and pulled my zipper down.

If you enjoyed this sample then look for **Naughty Wives**.

From the Author

WANT FREE COPIES OF MY BOOKS?
Just visit my blog and download free copies of my books:
awesomeauthors.org/justplainbob

Yes, I write about sluts and whores because as everyone knows, you tend to write about the things you know. And I do like sluts and whores, just not the ones that lie to me and cheat on me.

So be forewarned - if you click on a Just Plain Bob story you will be getting sluts, whores and husbands who do not kill, maim and destroy. There are other things you will rarely find in a Just Plain Bob story.

If you enjoyed any of my books then please share the love and promote my books in Amazon. I would really appreciate your honest reviews, too!

Good news is always welcome.

One Last Thing, For Kindle Readers...

When you turn the page, Kindle will give you the opportunity to rate this book and share your thoughts on Facebook and Twitter. If you enjoyed my writings, would you please take a few seconds to let your friends know about it? Because... when they enjoy they will be grateful to you and so will I.

Thank you!

Just Plain Bob
justplainbob@awesomeauthors.org

You may also like the books by these authors:

HIS WIFE *and* HER HUSBAND
SPOUSES WHO STRAY

HOT ROMANCE EROTICA
JACK RYDER

Shelly and I were always sort of mismatched now that I look back at the eight years we were husband and wife. I was always a night owl. Preferring the late night hours to write my stories when there were no distractions and the rest of the neighborhood was asleep.

Shelly was one of those early to rise and early to bed sorts. She spent her morning working out to keep her highly tuned body at its peak performance. She spent the rest of her day with her clients. Shelly was a very popular personal trainer in our little part of the world.

Things went fairly well the first three or four years of our relationship. We could laugh off our differences as amusing quirks that added to the uniqueness of our love. But after a while, those differences began to grate on us. It began to erode the foundation of that uniqueness.

Shelly was always so busy that she often left things a mess. It wasn't just a little mess either. She would leave any room she'd been in looking like a tornado had roared through. After years of cleaning up after her, I began to resent it. I felt like I was her personal maid or something.

It seemed that Shelly's biggest resentment was that I would try to get sexual with her when she was ready for bed. But she grew more and more resistant as the years went by. Often telling me she was too tired or that it pissed her off that I would get back up afterward to go do some more writing.

After a while, we fell into a routine of sorts. I stopped complaining about her messiness but became very quiet and uncommunicative when she was home. She responded by coming home later and later and curtailing our sex life to a holiday treat or as a favor when she wanted something special. Those episodes usually occurred each time I received a large bonus when one of my books did very well.

I'm sort of telling you all this boring stuff so you can get an idea of how we sort of drifted our own directions. I became accustomed to doing pretty much whatever I wanted to go do. And Shelly pretty much came and went as she pleased as well.

But you need to understand that I never once considered having an affair or seeking out companionship in any manner. I truly believed that we were just suffering through growing pains and that eventually things would straighten out for us.

I also have to tell you that I have a very active sexual drive. As time passed, I found ways to…take care of my own needs so to speak. I found ways to satisfy myself. I found there were many ways that one could have anonymous sex and there were many others that were seeking the same release.

It started out with a few harmless trips to the Adult Arcade out on the edge of town. The sign had just caught my eye one afternoon after having an argument with Shelly. She had taunted me afterward saying that the next time she would fuck me is when pigs fly.

I felt a little apprehensive when I first stepped into the arcade. Afraid I might see someone that I know and they would think I was some sort of pervert. I was surprised to see that there were nearly a dozen people milling around in the large center area that was filled with rows of videos, sex toys and sexy lingerie.

I noticed a couple of men over in the back corner by the gay magazine row. They seemed to be sizing me up as they gawked at the magazines they were holding. It even appeared that two of them were sort of petting each other below the level of the shelves.

There were a couple of middle age women that seemed like they were a little embarrassed to be here. But they were whispering requests at the counter clerk.

I figured they were here to purchase some stuff to spice up their sex life at home. I felt a little jealous as I thought of that. At least these women were trying to find ways to keep their sex life alive.

I also noticed one woman in the other back corner alone. She was holding up sexy panties as if inspecting them. But she kept looking over as if to see if I was paying attention to her. She was wearing a very short mini skirt and extremely tight pull over top. The way her nipples were poking against the tight cotton fabric, it was easy to tell she was not wearing a bra. She sort of looked like a hooker.

I noticed the hall way to the arcade with the private booths. I smiled at the woman one last time then made my way down the hall. I went to the very last booth at the far end of the hall and closed the door behind me. I quickly shoved $5 in the pay slot and selected a porn video to watch.

I just got my pants down and was gently tugging on my prick when I heard the door to the booth next to mine open and close. Moments later, I heard the sound of the machine taking money in the next booth. Then I heard a loud moaning as the porn came on in the next booth. In a few seconds, the sound became the same as the video that I was watching.

I was just getting a good rhythm to my jerking when I suddenly heard "Pssssst," coming from the wall next to me. When I glanced down, I saw a four inch hole in the wall at just the same level as my cock…

If you enjoyed this sample then look for His Wife and Her Husband.

Amy Redek

Farell

Hot Romance Erotica

'It was a dark and stormy night and the lightening crashed and the thunder flashed,' I began before being interrupted by a bright seven-year-old girl.

'Excuse me, Mr. Farrell,' her right arm held up high, 'but shouldn't that be the lightning flashed and the thunder crashed?'

'Quite right, my young Miss. I changed the words to see if you were paying attention,' which proved that at least one was. This was becoming my party piece as I was always invited to the birthday parties of my niece and nephew and as the end of the party was nigh, I would always be asked to tell a ghost story. The floor would be cleared and we would only have the light of a solitary candle on the mantel piece behind me as the children sat in a semi-circle before me, holding hands. So in the gloom of the room with just this single flickering light that didn't show my features, I had to make the most of the story with the tones of my voice. They liked it when it was deep and sonorous to try and portray that somewhere outside of our circle was a mysterious and threatening presence. One year I didn't begin with those words and I had cries of dismay, so ever since, I've had to begin my stories the same way. They understood these words whether it be around an old house alone in the middle of the moors, or a castle perched high on a cliff edge with the seas crashing and rolling against the sharp jagged rocks that had seen many ships founder. They could imagine the single flashing light high up in the castle, luring a ship to its destruction on the rocks below.

These were pictures they could conjure up in their mind's eye as I described the wind and the way that it talks to man, bird and beast. This was the beginning to their story and it was not to be left out though the critics say that a book should never open with these lines, but it was the way that my critics who sat before me all wanted it to begin.

But my own story for you really started with it being quite the opposite, though if I ever got to tell it to the children, it would have to be different. Spring had arrived and the sun was shining and all seemed right with the world. My name is Michael Farrell and I'm slightly overweight for my height of six foot if taken with my being thirty two years of age. I have light blue eyes, clean shaven, average features and have brown to black coloured hair which is of no value to the story but just helps to fill up the picture for you to see me.

I live alone in a cottage, of which there are twelve in what is known as Meadows Lane that leads nowhere from the lane at the top. This top lane, or road is one of those nightmare thoroughfares that only has passing areas about two hundred yards apart. Not lay-bys but just bits of ground where the hedge has been crushed over the years and were now just bare patches of earth that were full of mud and icy water during the winter. Many's the time you can hear the honking of horns as two vehicles meet and neither want to reverse to clear the way. It is usually the one with a female inside that finally gives way and makes the tricky job of reversing round a blind bend to be able to pull into the hedge lined gap.

This was the road at the top of my lane and it had just a small pub and one shop that sold a lot of nothing, and to complete this part of the village, there were six cottages either side of these two public places. These were all on the right as we came out and turned left from Meadows Lane because the land opposite and onto which my cottage backed, was Meadows Farm.

It was over a quarter of a mile before we came to the stables on the right and this was directly opposite another lane that ran in the same direction as the one I lived in. Now this would show the ingenuity of the district's planning many years ago, because it bounded the other side of Meadows Farm and that my lane was called Meadows Lane, they named this one by just dropping the letter S. Brilliant thinking on someone's part. This lane too had twelve cottages and so it was almost a mirror image to mine if one could look down from above.

Now at the bottom of the two lanes and of the farm in between, was what were locally known as the cliffs. A misnomer if ever there was one like calling our hamlet a village. Our cliffs were about twenty foot high and as the land and soil slowly broke away with wind and rain, they became slopes that ran down to a narrow pebbled beach, if I could even call it that. Though the land of the farm was flat where the farmhouse stood, it rose up towards the sea end but rolled down on either side to where the lanes were, so from where I lived, I couldn't see the lane on the other side of these fields because of this small hill.

I know, I know, you're getting impatient for me to start the story but I had to give you the lay out and topography of the place first and you'll understand why in a minute. Now I'll get to the problem I caused our postie, postman to you townies, his name by the way is Pat. Well, that is what everybody calls him like they call our village Toy Town. We don't have a Noddy but we do have a Big Ears, but due to the size of the fellow, no one has ever dared call him that. Built like a brick..., er, outhouse, with arms and shoulders that many a tree would be proud to have limbs like that. He was much in demand at harvest time because he could pitch fork even the most soggiest of hay bales to toss it over twenty feet high onto the hay wagon.

But the problem I caused our postman was of my surname Farrell, because there was another man of that name in the opposite lane, only his Christian name was Nicholas. When we did eventually meet, it became Mick and Nick, mine coming first alphabetically. What compounded postman Pat's problem was none of the cottages had numbers or names and he delivered by the surname on the letter, so sometimes I got Nick's and he got mine if the writer dropped the letter S. Also I think Pat had an eye problem to tell the difference between the two letters of our Christian names.

It was a joke when it first happened as I got a letter that was meant for Nick and so I took a walk along the cliffs and over the hill to hand deliver it myself for which he opened a bottle of beer as a thank you. Then another day he delivered one to me and I reciprocated with a bottle of beer and a chat. Now this would happen three, maybe four times a year so we both now always kept a few bottles of beer available in the pantry as payment.

It was on this glorious spring morning that Pat delivered one for Nick to my cottage, so after I had my breakfast and washed up and put the things away decided to take over his letter. I put it in my jacket pocket and went out into the garden but stopped as I looked at the sorry state of my roses. I saw that they could do with a bit of nutrient about now if I wanted a good showing this year, so decided to call in at the stables first to order some manure.

I walked up my lane and turned left and gave a wave to Dave, the pub landlord as he was seeing to his weekly delivery by the draymen. I ambled along the lane, keeping one ear cocked for the sound of any approaching vehicle from either direction, but as we are such a way off the beaten track, we don't get that many. I called in at the stables and spoke to the head lad; lad? He was nearly double my age and agreed to drop a couple of bags off at my cottage though I stressed that only when there was time and not to rush, which was a bit of a joke because nobody rushed in Toy Town.

With the manure ordered, I then went down the lane to Nick's cottage and I called out as I entered the garden but only got silence as a response. I went round to his back door which was never locked and went in, calling out his name again. The kitchen was clean and tidy but still no Nick. I went and felt the tea cloth and found that it was damp which told me he'd eaten and washed up. I went to his pantry and took out a bottle of beer and put it in the middle of the table so that it was a reminder of what he owed me as I propped his letter up against it.

I went out closing the door and down through his garden for the walk along the cliffs back to my place. It certainly was a pleasure to walk through the grass and feel the first hint of warmth from the sun on my back so I took my jacket off and slung it over my shoulder, enjoying the slight breeze coming off the sea and I could hear what I thought were larks as I got near the top of the small hill.

It was by looking up into the sky and not looking where I was putting my feet that I tripped and went sprawling flat down on my stomach, and as I raised my head, came face to face with Nick. There, in the grass, eyes half closed and the mouth fixed in a rictus of a grin, a foot away from me was Nick's head…

If you enjoyed this sample then look for **Farell**.

Ben E. Dorm

Mrs. MOON

ROMANCE EROTICA

Conversation ceased when Mrs Moon entered. She paused and looked around, letting them see her as she gave the place the once over. It hadn't altered at all to her notice: ill-fitting, threadbare carpet, once blue but faded and dirtied by years of traffic, mostly scuffed and dirty work boots, all raggedy at the periphery and curled in one corner. The same old calendar hung on the wall, a bosomy young blonde smiling out, the young woman at least two years older than the year displayed in the calendar's header. A knackered settee sat against the back wall, while a remnant from some ancient kitchen stood in one corner, a freestanding unit brought in by someone to act as a surface upon which rested a kettle, a five litre bottle of water, and the makings for tea and coffee. There was a fridge next to the kitchen unit, unloved and unclean, its job being to keep milk cold during the working week as well as lager for the Friday afternoon drink-up. A low coffee table was in front of the sofa, much be-ringed by coffee and tea stains, an overflowing ashtray in its geograph-ical centre despite the no-smoking sign on display.

"Hello, Mrs Moon," one of the men said, a stocky, grey-haired man, his hair cut very short to his scalp. The man pushed himself upright from where he'd been leaning against the fridge, his arms folding across his chest as he moved. Mrs Moon knew him to be in his late forties, the foreman of the workshop.

"Tim," she replied, acknowledging the greeting. She surveyed the assembled group, eying each in turn. "Hello, boys," she breathed.

Three of the four remaining men mumbled their hellos, the trio wearing the same garb as Tim, grease-stained, baggy overalls. They were ubiquitous twenty-something's, one of whom Mrs Moon found rather attractive. The other two were nondescript, longish dark hair in need of a trim. In Mrs Moon's eyes they were unremarkable in every way, except to serve as extra meat in Mrs Moon's diet. She couldn't even recall their names – Alan and Pete or some such. Anyway, she had no interest at all in their personal lives or their circumstances. The young mechanics were always changing, with one leaving to be replaced by another, Tim being a constant in all the months Mrs Moon had enjoyed her Thursday afternoon sojourn in their company. She nodded at the trio, two of whom were sitting in the questionable embrace of the sofa, knees high because of insubstantial support in the sway-backed piece of furniture, the good-looking one sitting on the seat of an old ladder-backed chair, his arms dangling over the back support, the chair reversed beneath him.

The fifth man, the one standing with his back to the rear wall, the man in the suit, she ignored completely.

"Are you ready?" Mrs Moon asked, moving into the room with an exaggerated swing of her hips. "I hope so," she added, facing square on to the sofa, fists on her hips. "Because I'm so fucking horny…"

If you enjoyed this sample then look for **Mrs. Moon**.

JOAN VEGAS

Hot Dates
Being Sandwiched
MFM AND RELATED ADVENTURES

HOT ROMANCE EROTICA

According to leading Sociologists, the number of American women who have opened their lives to intimate affairs has substantially increased in recent years. It is estimated that as many as 60% of all married women have had affairs. That's right... 60%!

Yes, that's still less than the estimated 70% of all married men who are believed to have had affairs, but it reflects the fact that growing numbers of women are reaching out for sexual variety in their lives.

Sadly, traditional secret affairs still usually bring with them feelings of guilt and anxiety. Yet, it is understandable that women, just like men, want their sensual lives to be fuller, they want "newness," and they want the excitement of experiencing different partners and different sexual adventures.

I have always been a proponent of variety in sexuality for both men and women. But, I have advocated that couples share in the development of new pleasures for each other, that they intentionally allow each other to experience extra partner and that they actively participate in providing extra partners "as gifts" for their primary partner.

Some call what I advocate "open marriage." While I feel open marriages are far better than the traditional "closed," monogamous marriage, I feel that husbands and wives can enhance the open marriage concept by periodically inviting others to join THEM in bedroom play. I encourage couples to explore the addition of another guy or gal to their love play as a way to take an active role in providing their spouse with extra partners while doubling that spouse's sensual pleasures.

For decades (centuries?) men have talked to their wives about bringing an extra guy to their shared bed. Many men fantasize about watching their wife being serviced by one or more other guys. Sometimes it is the woman who proposes such a threesome (MFM - male/female/male, or female-centered threesomes). But, more often than not, the wife is the "hesitant" party, turned-on by the idea, but "hesitant" to really give it a try.

The following are comments gleaned from letters I have received over the last few years from women who have opened their lives to extra partners... not within the context of affairs, but within the context of threesomes or open marriage agreements. I will let them tell for themselves WHY they enjoy this way of expanding their feminine potential.

Joan

If you enjoyed this sample then look for **<u>Hot Dates:</u> <u>Being Sandwiched</u>**.

WHITE CRAVING
for
BLACK

HOT EROTICA

SAMMY WEST

"Hi honey, come on in" Her hand reached out and I climbed in hearing the door swish shut behind me.

Sherie shared the back with 1 other, an older black guy wearing a suit, I guessed in his mid to late fifties, he said nothing as I flopped on the seat opposite him, his face expressionless and his eyes covered with dark sunglasses.

"How are you? This is Steve" she gushed as her palm gestured towards our fellow passenger.

The van suddenly jerked into life tinted glass partition separated us from our driver,

"I'm very well thanks" my voice took on a kind of squeaky tone as I felt my throat begin to dry suddenly, wondering what on earth I had let myself in for.

"Are you nervous? Nah don't be silly, it is going to be a great day for us all." Her enthusiasm seemed catching as a smile spread across my face.

Steve turned to her and whispered something in her ear,

"Honey could you just lift that dress a little for us" she asked before turning back to Steve.

I eased my dress up a little, lifting my bum from the seat enough so I could move it above my pull-ups and he nodded appreciatively.

"Well that's test 1 completed." Her dark puffy lips parted into another of her beaming smiles, revealing perfect white teeth.

Steve whispered once again, his face still emotionless, his eyes a mystery behind those gold-rimmed sunglasses.

"Time for test 2 already babe" she fixed my gaze then her eyes wandered to his crotch. I watched as her hands undid him and suddenly began to feel sick, my stomach in a knot as the reality began to unfold.

I had known all along this was not going to be some innocent little drinks party, I knew that it was inevitably going to involve some romp but now I started to realize that I was going to have very little say in the forthcoming events. In fact I doubted my opinion would even matter at all, thoughts raced through my mind as I watched her pull out a very dark, thick but flaccid manhood. She looked across and smiled, her eyes narrowing slightly giving her an almost menacing look.

He reached across with a long cane and tapped the end between my legs silently commanding me to part them, my lace covered pussy now in full view.

"Let's see you play with that white organ" The playfulness now disappeared from Sherie's voice.

I felt my mouth suddenly dry up, I knew that anything but a positive answer was futile and began to reach down between my legs his face remaining expressionless as my finger pulled aside my knickers exposing my dampening self..

If you enjoyed this sample then look for <u>White Craving For Black</u>.

WANT FREE COPIES OF MY BOOKS?
Just visit my blog and download free copies of my books:
awesomeauthors.org/justplainbob

www.ingramcontent.com/pod-product-compliance
Lightning Source LLC
Chambersburg PA
CBHW071410170626
46811CB00003B/1337